The Dinosaur
Who Roared for More

Russell Punter

Illustrated by Andy Elkerton

Sid runs a busy restaurant.

There's lots of food to try...

from steaming soup,

and veggie stew,

to smooth banoffee pie.

One day, Dora waddles in.
She just can't wait to eat.

Sid rushes up to welcome her
and shows her to a seat.

Dora starts with mushroom tart.
I'll love this dish,
I'm sure!

Dora chomps the tart down fast
and then she roars for...

MORE!

Dora eats tart number two.

Then three...

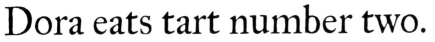

and four...

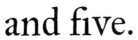

and five.

Minutes later, Sid returns.

I'll love this dish,
I'm sure!

Dora gobbles up the pie and then she roars for...

MORE!

Pies two and three,

then four,

then five,

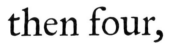

all vanish from
her plate.

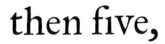

There goes six,
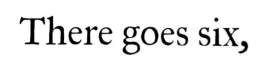

soon seven's gone,

and so has
number eight.

"I need dessert now," Dora says.
"My tummy mustn't rumble."

Sid brings her order
out at once.

One toffee apple crumble!

She guzzles up the crumble fast,
as custard hits the floor.

"That was yummy," she declares,
but then she roars for...

Crumbles two and three go down...

then four...

five, six

and seven.

Then number eight...

and nine...

and ten.

Says Dora,
"This is heaven!"

That should be fine till supper time.

I may be back for more.

But when she leaves to head for home...

She can't fit through the door!

Sid tries to help.

He bumps...

and shoves...

but he can't move
poor Dora.

"You've eaten too much food," he pants.
Stay here till you get smaller.

So Dora helps Sid serve his food...

She's on her feet all day.

She huffs and puffs and pants at first.

But soon she feels okay.

One week later, Dora's off.

She fits right through the door.

"I liked working here," she says.

"I'd like to work some more."

Now Dora has fun helping out.
She skips across the floor.

She eats good food,
but not too much...

and never roars for more!

Edited by Lesley Sims

This edition first published in 2022 by Usborne Publishing Ltd., Usborne House,
83-85 Saffron Hill, London EC1N 8RT, England. usborne.com Copyright © 2022, 2020 Usborne Publishing Ltd.